RECORD
RUN

BY JAKE MADDOX

illustrated by Sean Tiffany

text by Eric Stevens

Impact Books are published by Stone Arch Books
151 Good Counsel Drive, P.O. Box 669
Mankato, Minnesota 56002
www.stonearchbooks.com

Library of Congress Cataloging-in-Publication Data

Maddox, Jake.
    Record run / by Jake Maddox; text by Eric Stevens;
illustrated by Sean Tiffany
        p. cm. — (Impact books. A Jake Maddox sports story)
        ISBN 978-1-4342-1598-7
        [1. Track and field—Fiction.] I. Stevens, Eric, 1974-
II. Tiffany, Sean, ill. III. Title.
PZ7.M25643Rec 2010
[Fic]—dc22   2009004094

Summary:
After getting soaked by Harry's water balloon, Paul chases Harry down.
He didn't expect Harry to be so fast. He gives Harry a choice: join the
track team or else. Harry doesn't think it's fun to run if he's not being
chased. With Paul's help, can Harry find a good reason to run?

Creative Director: Heather Kindseth
Graphic Designer: Carla Zetina-Yglesias

Printed in the United States of America

TABLE OF
CONTENTS

CHAPTER 1

The Two-Pointer. 5

CHAPTER 2

The Chase 12

CHAPTER 3

Caught. 16

CHAPTER 4

Lunch 21

CHAPTER 5

First Practice. 28

CHAPTER 6

Not Good Enough. 34

CHAPTER 7

Boring 41

CHAPTER 8

Old Tricks. 45

CHAPTER 9

To Win. 52

CHAPTER 10

Personal Best 57

THE TWO-POINTER

Harry Ecker and Jeff Razz were laughing. The two sixth graders were crouched together in a jungle gym at a park near Polk Middle School.

The jungle gym they were hiding in was built to look like a pirate ship. At the top was a wood cabin.

From inside the cabin, Jeff and Harry could see the whole park, but no one could see them.

"Okay, Jeff," Harry said, still laughing. "That's three for you, and two for me."

"You know it," Jeff replied. "Looks like I'll win again."

A big pile of water balloons was next to the boys. Harry reached out and picked one up.

"You only have one throw left," Jeff said. "Even if you get someone soaking wet, you can only tie the score."

Harry thought for a second. "What if I score a two-pointer?" he asked.

Jeff laughed and shook his head. "You must be nuts," he said. "You have to soak an eighth grader to get two points. Are you really that crazy?"

Harry smiled. "I'll do whatever it takes to win," he said.

Jeff shrugged. "We'll see," he replied. "We can't wait all day for an eighth grader to walk by."

Harry slowly got to his knees and peeked through the window. He turned his head to look carefully over the whole park, trying to spot someone to throw the next water balloon at.

"There," Harry said, pointing.

Jeff got up and looked through the window. "Where?" he asked.

Harry was pointing toward the edge of the park. Two boys from their school, both eighth graders, were leaning against the fence.

"Look at them," Harry said. "They look like they're half asleep. They'll never know it was me."

Jeff laughed. "Maybe," he said. "But they're pretty far off. I bet you can't even reach them with a water balloon from here."

"Who said I have to throw it from here?" Harry said.

"What are you going to do, walk right up to them?" Jeff replied.

"If that's what it takes to win!" Harry said. He tossed the water balloon lightly in his hand. "So, are you going to come with me?"

Jeff shook his head. "No way, man," he said. "If you hit one of them, you win. But I'm staying right here where it's safe."

Harry shrugged. "Suit yourself," he said. Then he climbed down the ladder out of the cabin.

Harry took a few cautious steps toward the two eighth graders. He stopped behind a tree when he thought he was close enough.

Harry glanced back at the pirate ship cabin. He could see Jeff's face peeking through the window.

"Well, here goes nothing," Harry muttered to himself. Then he stepped out from behind the tree.

The two eighth graders were facing the other way and still seemed half asleep. Harry pulled back his arm. With all his might, he heaved the water balloon toward the two older boys.

The water balloon hit one of them right in the back and exploded. It sent a flood of water all over the boy.

Right away, Harry stepped back behind the tree to hide. If he started running, the eighth graders would easily spot him.

"Please, don't let them see me!" he whispered to himself.

"Hey!" a voice shouted. "Who threw that water balloon at me? You better come out now if you know what's good for you!"

Harry stayed completely still and silent. He listened carefully.

"I think I saw someone run behind that tree," another voice replied. "I bet it was him!"

"Oh yeah?" said the first voice again. "Let's go find out."

"Uh-oh," Harry whispered. He decided it was time to start running.

"Get him!" the first voice said again.

Harry glanced over his shoulder as he ran. One of the boys — the dry one — wasn't very fast. After a few seconds of running, he just stopped and caught his breath.

But the boy Harry had hit with the balloon was still chasing him. And he looked really mad!

CHAPTER 2

THE CHASE

Harry ran as fast he could. *At least this means I beat Jeff,* he thought as he ran. *I got more water-balloon points than he did.*

He managed to smile as he picked up speed. Harry didn't really know the eighth grader he'd hit. He had seen him around school, but otherwise he didn't know anything about the older boy.

It's not like he's going to beat me up or anything, Harry thought.

Still, Harry didn't want to get caught. It wouldn't feel like a real victory if he got caught. And Jeff would definitely make fun of him.

Harry glanced over his shoulder again. The kid was catching up. Harry tried to put on a little more speed.

Soon he reached the north end of the park. But suddenly he realized something. He hadn't been paying attention to where he was going.

He wasn't thinking as he ran, and he forgot the north end of the park didn't have a gate. Harry was running at full speed, right at a three-foot fence!

"Uh-oh," he muttered to himself. "Guess I have no choice, though. I'm going to have to jump it."

Just before he ran smack into the fence, Harry took an extra deep breath. Then he jumped as far and high as he could. He cleared the fence so easily, he even surprised himself.

"Stop!" the boy behind him called.

Harry kept running. He was sure the eighth grader would stop at the fence. When Harry glanced behind him, though, he saw the older boy glide effortlessly over the fence.

"Whoa," Harry said as he ran on. He was starting to get tired now.

After a few more steps, he felt something tug on his collar. He was pulled to a stop.

"Gotcha!" the older boy said with a huff.

Harry was caught!

CHAPTER 3

CAUGHT

"Get your hands off me!" Harry said. He spun around and managed to get his shirt out of the older boy's hand.

"Take it easy, man," the eighth grader replied. "I'm not going to hurt you."

"I almost got away," Harry said.

"Yeah, I noticed," the eighth grader replied. "Why'd you throw that water balloon at me? I don't even know you."

Harry shrugged. "It's a game I play with my friend," he said. "We get a point for each kid we hit with a balloon. But we get two points if we hit an eighth grader."

"I see," the older boy said. "So you got two points for me?"

Harry smiled. "That's right," he said. "In fact, I beat Jeff by a point thanks to that hit."

"Well, at least I was the winning attack," the older boy replied. "Truth is, I was going to drag you by the collar to the kiddie pool and drench you."

"So what's stopping you?" Harry asked, frowning. "You caught me."

The older boy laughed. "To be honest, I didn't think you'd put up such a good chase," he said.

"What do you mean?" Harry asked.

"You're fast," the boy replied. "And I can't believe how easily you got over that fence. It was pretty amazing."

Harry shrugged again. "It was easy," he said. "So you're not going to soak me?

The other boy shook his head. Then he looked at Harry and frowned. "What's your name?" he asked.

"Harry Ecker," Harry replied.

The older boy said, "Harry Ecker, I'm Paul Carson. And I won't soak you on one condition."

Harry squinted at Paul. "What's that?" he asked.

"After a run like that, what else?" Paul said. "You have to join the Polk Middle School track team."

"The track team?" Harry said. "You must be kidding. I'm only in sixth grade. No one makes it onto a sports team in sixth grade, except the special B squads."

"Don't worry about that," Paul said. "I'm the team captain. When I tell Coach Norman how fast you are, he'll let you on the team. I have no doubt about it."

Harry looked at his feet. "Can I think about it?" he said, looking up.

"Sure," Paul said. "Let me know tomorrow. But my friends and I will be ready with about a hundred water balloons. And we'll be right outside the school at three tomorrow if I don't hear from you before then."

Harry nodded. "Okay, I got it," he said. "You'll hear from me before then."

CHAPTER 4

LUNCH

The next day at lunch, Harry dropped his tray next to Jeff's on the table.

"This is so lame," Harry said. Angrily, he sat down in the plastic chair.

"What is?" Jeff asked. "It's pizza roll day. This is so not lame." Jeff popped a pizza roll into his mouth and savored it slowly.

"Not the pizza rolls," Harry replied. "I mean the track team thing."

Jeff nodded and swallowed his bite. "Oh, right," he said. "That. Well, so join the team. It's not like you have to try hard once you're on the team or anything."

"What do you mean? Do you think I should agree to join?" Harry asked. "And then show up to practice, but not make any effort?"

Jeff nodded. He sipped his juice. "Sure," he said. "Paul just said you have to join, right? You don't have to win a medal. Or break all the school records or anything."

Harry nodded slowly. "That's true," he said. He glanced at the clock. Then he went on, "I guess I should go and find Paul. I'll be in class the rest of the day. Then, at three, he's going to drench us if I don't find him first."

"Us?" Jeff repeated. He gasped. "What do you mean? How did I get involved in this?"

Harry got out of his seat. He replied, "Well, we usually leave school together. And if that happens, I have a feeling you'll be in the line of fire."

"In that case, good luck, bro," Jeff said. He popped another pizza roll into his mouth. "You'll make a great jock!"

Jeff laughed as Harry walked off to find Paul. Harry tried not to let it get to him.

* * *

Harry had a good idea where to find Paul. Most of the eighth-grade jocks ate lunch in the courtyard. He'd look there first.

Harry pushed open the courtyard doors and stepped into the sun.

He squinted for a minute and shaded his eyes. Looking back and forth, he scanned the crowd of kids eating at the plastic picnic tables.

"Hey, Harry!" someone called out. "You looking for me?"

Harry turned and spotted Paul waving at him. The eighth grader was sitting with five other kids, including two girls. Harry didn't know any of their names.

Harry waved back and started walking over. At the same time, Paul jumped up. He jogged toward Harry. The other kids at the table laughed a little when they saw Harry.

"So, have you made up your mind?" Paul asked. "You ready to be our next track star or what?"

Harry thought one more minute.

Do I really want to give up my afternoons and join the track team? he thought. *Or should I just take my soaking and get on with my life?*

Harry frowned, thinking about it. *Then again,* he thought, *I don't think I want every jock in the school to spend the rest of the year soaking me with water balloons every time they see me.*

"I guess I've made up my mind," Harry finally said. "I'll join the middle school track team."

"Excellent!" Paul said. He put out his hand for a high five.

Harry threw up his hands. "I can't promise I'm going to be a track star, you know," he said. "I'll be the youngest on the team."

Paul smiled and shook his head. "No worries," he said. "I've seen you run. Just show up at the track today at four, okay? I'll talk to Coach Norman."

Harry nodded. "Okay, I'll be there then," he said.

If I have to, he added to himself.

CHAPTER 5

FIRST PRACTICE

A few minutes before four o'clock, Jeff and Harry stood at the back door of the school. They could see the track at the far end of the field. Lots of kids were standing around in red and gold uniforms. Most of them were stretching or jogging in place.

"Those are some goofy-looking uniforms," Jeff said. He shook his head slowly. "I wouldn't be caught dead in one of those."

Harry looked down at his own uniform. Paul had given it to him. "Well, you don't have to join the team," Harry replied, "so bug off."

"Hope it's not too bad," Jeff said. "Have fun." He popped some gum into his mouth and walked off.

"Yeah, I'm sure I will," Harry replied under his breath. Then he started jogging across the field toward the track.

"Here he comes, Coach," Paul was saying as Harry jogged up. "That's Harry Ecker. He's the one I told you about."

Harry stopped in front of Paul and the coach. "Hi," he said nervously.

"Okay, Ecker," Coach Norman said. "You don't look so tough to me. Paul says you're fast."

Harry shrugged. "Yeah, I guess I'm pretty fast," he said.

"He's definitely fast, Coach," Paul added. "I saw this kid run a 400 meter — with hurdles — in under a minute the other day."

The coach raised his eyebrows. "Under a minute?" he repeated, surprised. "That would be impressive."

The coach looked at Harry again. "Okay, son," Coach Norman said. "I'll give you a shot, if Paul says you're up to it. I'll bring a uniform for you tomorrow. For today, just pay attention and do your best."

With that, the coach walked off. He stood in the center of the track and blew his whistle. All the team members stopped their warm-ups and gathered around.

Paul headed toward the group. Harry grabbed Paul by the wrist to stop him. "Hey, what was that all about?" Harry asked.

"What do you mean?" Paul replied.

"That stuff about a 400 meter and hurdles," Harry explained. "I don't even know what that means! There's no way you ever saw me run it."

Paul laughed. "You'll find out what it means pretty soon," he said. "But I was talking about yesterday, Harry. That chase you led me on was about 400 meters. And you cleared that fence like it was nothing! Just like a hurdler. You're a natural!"

Paul laughed again. Then he headed over to the coach with the other team members.

Harry stood where he was for a moment. As he looked at the track team, he thought, *Maybe I will be good at this track stuff after all.*

CHAPTER 6

NOT GOOD ENOUGH

"Okay, Ecker," Coach Norman said. "Let's talk."

The other runners had already split off into groups after a short talk from the coach. But Harry hadn't been sure which group he was supposed to join.

"Carson says you're a 400 man," the coach said.

"I guess so," Harry replied.

"Okay then," the coach went on. He glanced at his clipboard. Then he pointed at a group of guys. "Head over there, with group B. They'll be running single lap drills."

"Single lap drills. Okay," Harry said.

"One lap is 400 meters, Ecker," Coach replied. "You have run a lap before, right?"

"Of course I have," Harry replied. "No problem."

The coach nodded. "Off you go," he said. Then he walked away to watch the team practice.

Harry jogged over to group B and joined them. There were about ten other guys getting ready to run the single lap drills.

"Hey, new kid," one of the runners said. "Are you going to run 400s?"

Harry nodded. "I guess so," he said.

"Okay then," the other boy said. "Line up. You can run with the first crew. We'll keep your time. Go on the whistle."

"Okay," Harry replied. He walked over to the other boys at the start line and stood with them.

"Ready!" shouted the boy who had shown Harry where to go. "Set!"

The other boys on the start line crouched down a little. Harry tried to copy them.

An instant later, the whistle blew. The runners shot off the line. Harry was a little slow to start, but he got up to speed pretty quickly.

Harry did his best to stay with the other runners. He watched them and copied their running style.

This is a long run, he thought. *There's no way Paul chased me that far yesterday.*

Just looking at how big the track was made him feel totally exhausted. He felt himself slowing down. With every step he took, he heard his feet slapping the weird rubbery pavement of the track.

It seemed like forever before he reached the finish line. He managed to beat a few of the other runners he'd started with.

"One minute, fifteen seconds," the boy at the finish called as Harry ran by. Coach Norman was waiting at the finish line too.

"Not too bad, Ecker," the coach said. "You're definitely a strong runner, especially for a sixth grader."

"Thanks, Coach," Harry replied, smiling. He was feeling pretty proud.

"Still, a minute fifteen isn't exactly under a minute," Coach Norman added. "Paul said you could run the 400 in less than sixty seconds. You're not going to make a liar out of my team captain, are you?"

Harry swallowed. "Um, no, Coach," he said. "I promise."

"All right then," the coach replied. Then he walked off to check on the guys doing high jumps.

Suddenly someone grabbed Harry's shoulder.

"Hey!" Harry said, spinning around. It was Paul.

"What gives, man?" Paul asked.

"What? What are you talking about?" Harry said.

"I told him you were fast," Paul replied. "You didn't really put on the speed out there today, did you?"

Harry shrugged. "I don't know," he said.

Paul took a deep breath and sighed. "Well," he said, "I know you're faster than that. You were probably just nervous. You'll do better next time."

With that, Paul walked off.

What does he know? Harry thought. *I never said I could run anyway.*

CHAPTER 7

BORING

That Saturday, Jeff sat at Harry's computer. "This game is awesome," Jeff said. A loud, wicked laugh came from the computer speakers.

"What happened?" Harry asked.

"Ah, he beat me again," Jeff said.

"You'll figure it out," Harry said. "Just try again." Harry lay down on his bed and started flipping through a new comic book.

"Hey, how's track going, anyway?" Jeff asked. "Did you go to practice every day this week?"

Harry nodded, but he didn't look up from the comic he was reading. "Yeah, I went," he said. "It's pretty boring, though."

"Really?" Jeff asked, surprised. "Aren't you the next big track star yet?"

Harry shrugged. "No way, man," he said. "Besides, like I said, it's boring. All you do is run in a circle like a hundred times."

"Yeah, that does sound boring," Jeff said. "I mean, if you're not being chased, why run as hard as you can? You might as well take it easy."

Suddenly Jeff pounded wildly at the keyboard of Harry's computer.

"Man, be careful with my keyboard!" Harry said, getting up.

"Sorry," Jeff said. "I almost won that time."

Harry shook his head. "There's no game you can play as well as I can, is there?" he asked with a chuckle.

Jeff leaned forward again. "That sounds like a challenge to me!" he said. He started up the game again.

Harry just laughed and went back to reading his comic.

CHAPTER 8

OLD TRICKS

After the weekend, Harry wasn't looking forward to track practice. At three o'clock on Monday afternoon, he and Jeff headed through the rear exit of Polk Middle School.

Harry stopped and looked at the track across the field. "Ugh," he said. "Another day of track practice." He shook his head. "I am not looking forward to this," he added.

"Don't you want to go?" Jeff asked.

Harry shrugged. "Not really," he replied. "I think I'll skip it, in fact. Let's go to the park for a few minutes."

"And do what?" Jeff said. "I'm all out of water balloons."

Harry smiled. "I've got about a hundred in my bag," he said. "We're all set."

"Nice," Jeff replied. The two headed across the grass toward the park.

* * *

Forty-five minutes later, Harry spotted Paul running through the park, carrying his track uniform.

"He must have forgotten that at home," Harry told Jeff. They were sitting in the pirate ship jungle gym, hidden from view. "He's way late for practice," Harry went on. "He's going to be in huge trouble."

"Hit him with a balloon!" Jeff suggested.

Harry laughed, a little too loudly. Paul stopped and looked up.

At that moment, Harry tossed a water balloon right at Paul. He missed, but the water balloon exploded on the ground near Paul's feet. It splashed his sneakers.

Paul looked up at the pirate ship jungle gym again. "Harry!" he called out. "Come down from there."

Harry peeked over the wall of the ship's cabin. "What's up?" he said with a laugh.

"It's almost four," Paul replied. "Aren't you going to practice?"

Harry shrugged. "Nah," he said. "I don't think so. It's really boring. And besides, my times haven't been very good. I don't think Coach Norman will miss me."

Paul was about to start arguing, but Harry raised his arm and whipped another water balloon over the wall.

It shot right past Paul and hit a high school boy who was walking through the park. It splattered water all over the boy's pants.

"High school boy!" Harry whispered. "That's got to be at least four or five points."

"Hey!" the high school boy shouted. He turned and eyed Paul. "Did you throw that balloon at me?" the high school boy asked.

Paul shook his head. "No way. Wasn't me!" he insisted. Harry and Jeff laughed. Paul looked up at the pirate ship.

The high school boy looked up at the pirate ship cabin too.

"Who's up there?" the high school boy asked loudly.

"Uh-oh," Jeff and Harry said together.

The high school boy started running toward them.

"You better run, Harry," Paul said, looking up the ladder.

"Oh, man," Harry said. He climbed down the ladder as fast as he could. "Here we go again!"

Harry took off like a shot. He ran right at the fence at the far end of the park. With ease, he leapt over the fence.

The high school boy was much older and bigger than Harry. Harry thought for sure the older boy would be able to clear the fence too.

But in midair, the older boy's sneaker caught on the top of the fence and he took a tumble onto the grass. He quickly got up and brushed himself off, but by then Harry was out of sight.

Paul followed close behind and soon caught up to Harry. "Harry," he called out. "Come to practice."

"Why?" Harry replied. "I'm no good. The coach said himself that my time on the 400 wasn't good enough. And I'd rather go home and play video games or hang out at the park with Jeff."

"I know you can run like a record breaker," Paul replied. "That chase was more proof! Just give it one more chance."

CHAPTER 9

TO WIN

Harry stood, catching his breath, for a moment. He glanced over Paul's shoulder to make sure the high school boy wasn't chasing him anymore.

The coast was clear.

"I don't know, Paul," Harry said. "I need a reason to run. It's like my friend Jeff said. If I'm not being chased, what's the point in running?"

Paul nodded. "So you need a good reason," he said. "Well, why do you do anything?"

"What do you mean?" Harry asked.

Paul pointed at the pirate ship jungle gym. "Why do you throw water balloons?" he asked.

Harry shrugged. "It's fun," he said. "Besides, I always get more points than Jeff." He smiled.

"What about those video games?" Paul asked. "What's your reason for that?"

"Finishing them," Harry replied. "Once I finish a game a couple of times, I don't usually play it anymore."

"You can finish a video game?" Paul asked.

"Of course," Harry answered. "That's how you win."

"So nothing is fun for you," Paul said, "unless you can win? You sure do love to compete."

Harry thought for a second. "I guess so," he replied.

Paul glanced at his watch. "We need to get to practice," he said. "But I have two things you should think about. Meets and personal bests."

"What do you mean?" Harry said. He followed Paul toward the boys' locker room.

"Competition!" Paul said. "It's what you thrive on!"

Harry thought about that. "Okay," he said slowly.

"Just for today," Paul added quickly, "I'm going to run the 400 drills with you."

"Why?" Harry asked. "You're a miler, aren't you?"

"Just for today," Paul repeated. "I have an idea."

CHAPTER 10

PERSONAL BEST

Harry and Paul were only a few minutes late to practice. They jogged over to the 400 group.

"Paul, you're in the wrong group," one of the 400-meter runners said. "Shouldn't you be training with the other milers?"

"I'm training with you guys for today," Paul replied.

The others glanced at each other. "Whatever you say," one of them said.

"If it's all right with you guys," Paul added, "the first drill will be just me and Harry with a full lap."

The others said that was okay. Harry and Paul stepped up to the start line.

"Harry, you take the outside lane," Paul said. "I'll take the inside behind you."

"You want me to start ahead of you?" Harry asked. "That's not fair."

"No," Paul replied. "The outside lane always starts a few feet ahead to make up for the curve in the track. If you're on the outside, you have to run a little bit further to make it around the curve than the person on the inside does."

"Oh, I get it," Harry said.

"Besides," Paul added, "this way I can chase you."

Harry took off at the whistle. He heard Paul's footsteps close behind him.

"Better not let me catch you," Paul taunted.

Harry kicked up his speed a little. He could tell Paul was falling farther behind. Harry smiled as he rounded the last curve.

The finish line was in sight.

Harry glanced over his shoulder. He could see that Paul was about five meters behind him. Harry was easily going to win!

Harry stepped over the finish line. Paul crossed the line a few seconds later. Coach Norman was right there with his clipboard. As Harry stopped to catch his breath, he listened for his time.

"One minute two seconds," called out the boy with the stopwatch.

Harry slowed to a walk and strolled back toward the coach. Paul asked, "How'd I do?"

The timer called out, "One minute and five seconds."

"Nice job, Harry," Coach Norman said. "That's your personal best time."

"Thanks, Coach," Harry replied.

Coach Norman looked at Paul. "I guess he is as good as you say he is," the coach said. "I bet he'll be able to run the 400 in a minute before we know it. Might get him under a minute yet."

Coach Norman winked at Harry. Then he walked off to check out the sprinters.

"Nice going, Harry," Paul said. "I knew you just needed some motivation."

"Thanks," Harry replied. "But you can't chase me in every race!"

"Now you can chase yourself," Paul said.

"Chase myself?" Harry asked, confused. "What are you talking about?"

"Don't you get it?" Paul said. "Last week, your best time was a minute and eleven seconds, right?"

"Right," Harry said.

"Today, you ran one minute and two seconds," Paul went on. "If you keep at it, you can shave another couple of seconds off that score."

"You mean get an even better time?" Harry said.

"Right," said Paul.

"So my only competition," Harry concluded, "is myself."

"The best competition there is," Paul added.

Harry nodded. "I can do that," he said. "I'm the only competition I need!"

ABOUT THE AUTHOR

Eric Stevens lives in St. Paul, Minnesota. He is studying to become a middle-school English teacher. Some of his favorite things include pizza, playing video games, watching cooking shows on TV, riding his bike, and trying new restaurants. Some of his least favorite things include olives and shoveling snow.

ABOUT THE ILLUSTRATOR

When Sean Tiffany was growing up, he lived on a small island off the coast of Maine. Every day, from sixth grade until he graduated from high school, he had to take a boat to get to school. When Sean isn't working on his art, he works on a multimedia project called "OilCan Drive," which combines music and art. He has a pet cactus named Jim.

GLOSSARY

cautious (KAW-shuhss)—if you are cautious, you try to avoid mistakes and danger

drench (DRENCH)—to make something completely wet

effortlessly (EF-urt-less-lee)—without trying

exhausted (eg-ZAWST-id)—very tired

heaved (HEEVD)—threw

impressive (im-PRESS-iv)—thought highly of by others

jock (JOK)—someone who plays sports

natural (NACH-ur-uhl)—a person who is good at something because of a special talent or ability

squad (SKWAD)—a team

victory (VIK-tuh-ree)—a win in a contest or battle

MORE ABOUT
FAMOUS RUNNERS

Between 1979 and 1996, **Carl Lewis** won 10 Olympic medals, including 9 gold medals. He also won 10 World Championship medals, including 8 gold medals. The International Olympic Committee awarded him the Sportsman of the Century honor, and Sports Illustrated named him Olympian of the Century. Lewis is most famous for his sprinting, both in individual events and as a member of a relay team.

Archie Hahn was the author of the book *How to Sprint*. Born in 1880, Hahn was one of the best sprinters of the first half of the 20th century. In the 1904 Olympics, held in St. Louis, Missouri, Hahn won three gold medals, in the 60 meter race, the 100 meter race, and the 200 meter race. Two years later, at a special Olympics known as the Intercalated Games, Hahn won the gold medal in the 100 meter race. He died in 1955.

Michael Johnson, a sprinter, won 4 Olympic gold medals and 9 world championships. He holds the world record for the 400 meter race and the 4 x 400 meter relay. One of the things Johnson is most famous for is his unique running style. While most runners take long strides and lift their legs, Johnson takes very short steps and keeps his body very upright.

Ryan Hall is a young runner from California. In 2008, at the age of 25, he placed tenth in the Olympic marathon in Beijing. It took Hall 2 hours, 12 minutes, and 33 seconds to run the 26.2 mile race. Earlier that year, he won the American Olympic Team Trials marathon in New York City, with a time of 2 hours, 9 minutes, and 2 seconds. His fastest time ever running a marathon was the London marathon in 2006. That year, it took him 2 hours, 6 minutes, and 17 seconds.

DISCUSSION QUESTIONS

1. Why did Harry join the track team?
   What else could he have done to keep
   Paul from being mad at him?

2. Harry says that kids his age never make
   the sports teams. What happens at your
   school? Do kids your age play sports?
   What sports do they play?

3. Harry and his best friend made up the
   water balloon game. What games do
   you play with your friends?

WRITING PROMPTS

1. At the beginning of this book, Harry spends a lot of time with his best friend. Write about your best friend.

2. Harry doesn't think he'll be good at the track team. Write about a time you tried something you weren't sure you'd be good at. What did you try? What happened?

3. Harry hits Paul with a water balloon. What if he had hit someone else? Write a story in which Harry hits someone else with the water balloon. How would things be different?

BOOKS
FOR EVERY
ATHLETE

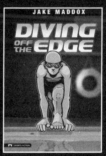

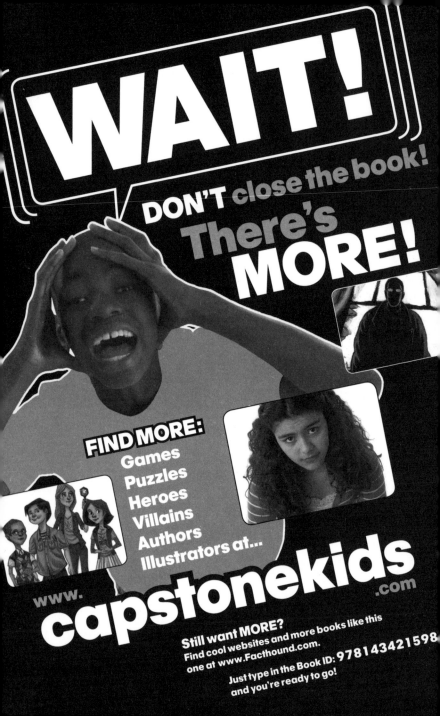